Davy   Kiki   Eddie

First published in the United States, Great Britain, Canada, Australia, and New Zealand
in 2006 by North-South Books, an imprint of NordSüd Verlag AG, Gossau Zürich, Switzerland.

Distributed in the United States by North-South Books Inc., New York.
Library of Congress Cataloging-in-Publication Data is available.
A CIP catalogue record for this book is available from The British Library.
ISBN-13: 978-0-7358-2048-7 / ISBN-10: 0-7358-2048-1
10 9 8 7 6 5 4 3 2 1

Printed in Belgium

Stay in Bed, Davy

By Brigitte Weninger
Illustrated by Eve Tharlet
Translated by Marianne Martens

NORTH-SOUTH BOOKS

NEW YORK / LONDON

One bright summer day,
Davy came sobbing to his mother.
"I feel awful!" he cried.
"Oh, dear," said Mother Rabbit worriedly.
"Did you eat something bad?"
Davy thought about what he'd eaten that day.
He had been pretty busy gobbling up some
blackberries before the others discovered the
bush. But he knew the berries weren't bad,
even though a few of them *were* still green.

Mother tucked Davy into his bed with a hot water bottle.
"Well, I guess we won't be able to go to Grandma's house today,"
said Father Rabbit. "It's too bad, because she is baking one of
her famous blackberry pies."
"Oh, no!" said Donny. "I love Grandma's blackberry pie!"
When Davy heard the word "blackberry," he put his hand over
his mouth and gagged.
"Shhhh! Can't you see how sick Davy is?" said Dan.

Just then, Davy's friend Eddie arrived.

"Hi Davy! My cousin Kiki is here visiting. Want to come play with us?"

"Davy can't go outside. He's sick," said Daisy.

"That's why we can't go to Grandma's and eat blackberry pie,"
Donny added sadly.

"Poor Davy," squeaked little Dinah. "Poor Dinah!"

"Eddie and I could stay here and look after Davy," suggested Kiki.

"If there's a problem, Eddie can run and get his mother."

Davy's brothers and sisters cheered. "Yeah! Great idea!"
Even Father agreed. "Kiki's idea sounds good to me."
"All right," said Mother. "But Davy, you must promise me
that you will stay in bed. Promise?"
Davy nodded. "I will," he said. "Bunny's promise."
The Rabbit family headed out happily. "Feel better, Davy!"
they called. "We'll be back this evening!"

"Playing will make you feel better!"
said Eddie.
"Let's make a stuffed bunny slide."
  But the first slide ended with a big splash.
"Oh, no! Poor Nicky!" cried Davy.
"Don't worry," said Kiki. "The tea was just
  lukewarm, so Nicky didn't get burned.
  We'll put him out in the sun to dry."
"I can't be sick without Nicky," protested
  Davy. "He makes me feel better. But I
  promised Mother I'd stay in bed."
"That's right," agreed Eddie. "And how
  can you stay in bed and be outside at the
  same time?"
  Suddenly Davy sat up. "*I* know how!
  Mother didn't say *where* the bed had to
  stay," said Davy, grinning.

So Kiki and Eddie dragged Davy's bed outside.
"Put it there, under the tree," said Davy. "We can make a tent!"
Davy put Nicky in the sun to dry. Eddie brought Davy some
crackers and Kiki got some fresh water for him.
"I feel better already," said Davy. "Fun and fresh
air really do help you get well. It's a shame we
can't play down by the stream today."

"Sure we can, we'll just carry you down there," said Kiki.

"That's really far," Eddie complained.

"Don't worry," said Kiki. "If Davy just holds his breath,
 he won't be so heavy."

"Phew! What a job!" panted Eddie when they reached the stream.
 He leaned against the bed, and suddenly, SPLASH!

The bed slid right into the stream!
"Oh, great," said Eddie, surprised. "I meant to do that. I think."
Davy was delighted. "Ahoy there, mateys! Now we have a real
boat. Come aboard, pirates!"
Kiki and Eddie grabbed a couple of
branches and climbed aboard
the pirate ship.

The pirates sailed the seas all afternoon.
But suddenly Davy sat up in panic.
"Oh, no! The sun is setting! We have to
hurry back before my family gets home!"

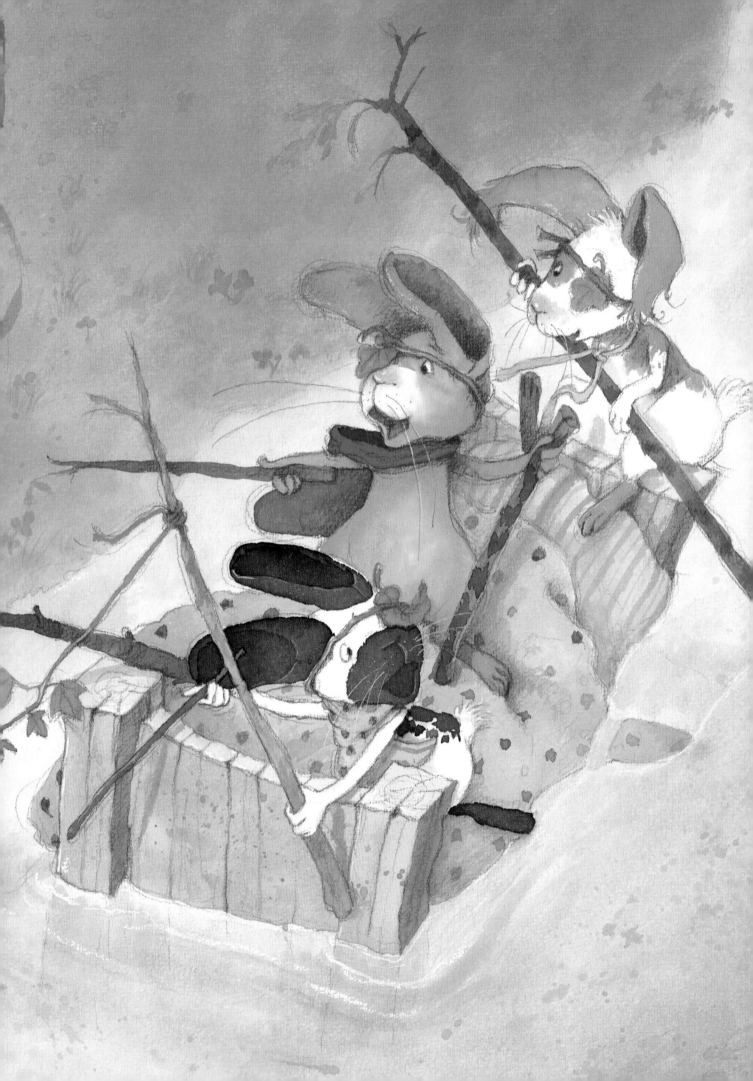

Kiki and Eddie paddled to shore and dragged the pirate ship out of the stream. Davy's bed had absorbed a lot of water and was much, much heavier now. Kiki and Eddie groaned under the load, while Davy cheered them on. "Quick, quick, hurry!" They had just managed to push the bed back into its place when Davy's family returned.
"Hello, we're back, and we brought you nurses some delicious blackberry pie!"

Davy was very happy. "Mmmm. Yummy! Can I have some pie, too?"

"You seem to be feeling much better," Father said with a smile. "Kiki and Eddie, you've been great nurses. Thank you!"

Mother Rabbit asked Davy, "Did you really stay in bed the whole time?"

Davy nodded eagerly. "Yes, I did, Mother. Bunny's promise!"

Mother stroked Davy's ear. "All right then, since you were a good little bunny, you may have some pie. But your friends look a little pale—I hope they haven't caught something from you." Kiki and Eddie shook their heads. "No, we're just tired. We'll see you tomorrow, Davy."

"Bye," Davy called after them. "Thanks for a great day, and be sure to stay in bed until you feel better!"